E-CIGARETTES AFFECTING LIVES

BY JEANNE MARIE FORD

Published by The Child's World®
1980 Lookout Drive • Mankato, MN 56003-1705
800-599-READ • www.childsworld.com

Photographs ©: iStockphoto, cover, 1, 6, 15, 16, 18, 22, 24; Red Line Editorial, 5; Shutterstock Images, 8, 11, 20; Media Photos/iStockphoto, 10; J. Michael Jones/iStockphoto, 12; Fang Xia Nuo/iStockphoto, 27; Steve Heap/Shutterstock Images, 28

Copyright © 2021 by The Child's World®
All rights reserved. No part of this book may be reproduced or utilized in any form or by any means without written permission from the publisher.

ISBN 9781503844872 (Reinforced Library Binding)
ISBN 9781503846401 (Portable Document Format)
ISBN 9781503847590 (Online Multi-user eBook)
LCCN 2019957957

Printed in the United States of America

Some names and details have been changed throughout this book to protect privacy.

CONTENTS

FAST FACTS 4

CHAPTER ONE
His 11th Finger 7

CHAPTER TWO
From Smoking to Vaping 13

CHAPTER THREE
A Costly Habit 19

CHAPTER FOUR
Explosive Vaping 25

Think About It 29
Glossary 30
To Learn More 31
Selected Bibliography 31
Index 32
About the Author 32

FAST FACTS

What It Is
- Vaping is inhaling an **aerosol**, popularly called a **vapor**.
- E-cigarettes, sometimes called vape pens, are a device used for vaping.
- Most e-cigarettes contain **nicotine**. Nicotine is toxic and highly **addictive**.

How It's Used
- E-cigarettes are filled with liquid chemicals called e-juice.
- A battery or plug supplies electricity to the e-cigarette. This powers a heating unit that turns the liquid into an aerosol.

Physical Effects
- The vapor contains many toxic chemicals. These have been linked to heart and lung disease as well as cancer.
- As of late 2019, more than 30 people had died from lung injuries that were connected to e-cigarette use.

Mental Effects
- Some e-cigarettes contain a chemical called THC. In young people, THC can cause problems with thinking and memory.

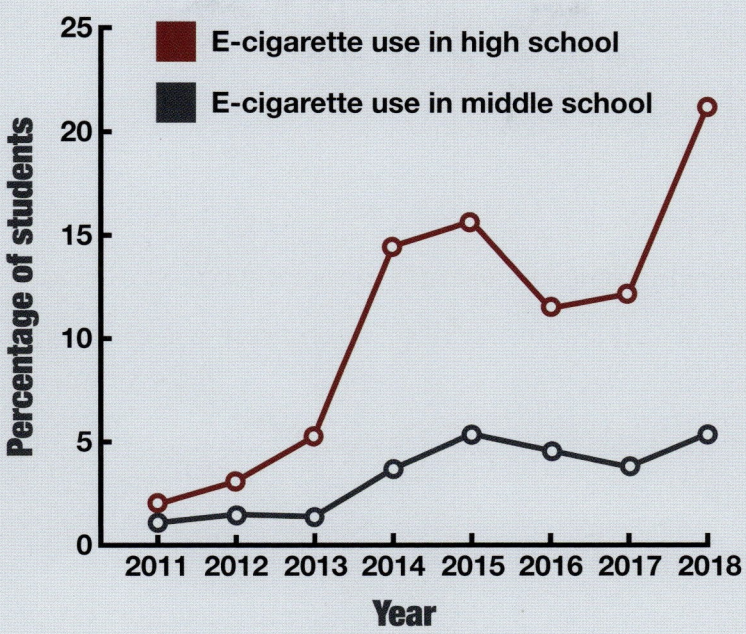

Cullen, Karen A. et al. "Use of Electronic Cigarettes and Any Tobacco Product Among Middle and High School Students–United States, 2011–2018." *Morbidity and Mortality Weekly Report*, 16 Nov. 2018, cdc.gov. Accessed 28 Oct. 2019.

Since 2011, e-cigarette use among middle schoolers and high schoolers has gone up. It surged between 2017 and 2018.

- ▶ Nicotine **withdrawal** can cause irritability and intense **cravings**.
- ▶ Nicotine addiction is especially harmful in young people. The earlier a person gets addicted, the harder it can be to quit.
- ▶ Vaping can make people more likely to become addicted to other harmful drugs.

CHAPTER ONE

HIS 11TH FINGER

Connor and his friends crowded into a basement for a party. Hip-hop music blared from speakers. They danced. Someone handed Connor an e-cigarette and urged him to try it. Connor did not drink or use drugs. He had never smoked cigarettes. He knew they were dangerous. People said vaping was safer.

The e-cigarette was small. Connor thought it looked like a flash drive. He took a puff. The vapor tasted like mint. He let it fill his lungs. He felt a sudden rush of **euphoria**.

Connor started taking quick puffs of his friends' e-cigarettes at school. A few weeks later, his family went on vacation. He missed the feeling vaping gave him. When he came back from vacation, Connor wanted his own e-cigarette. But he was not old enough to buy e-cigarettes.

◄ **Teenagers and young adults are the largest group of e-cigarette users.**

▲ **E-cigarette companies often use bold or colorful packaging to attract customers.**

He asked his friends if they could get him one. They could, but it would be illegal. It cost Connor $100.

Soon, Connor carried his own e-cigarette all the time. He called it his 11th finger. He spent all of his birthday and Christmas money on e-cigarettes.

At soccer practice, Connor noticed he was feeling breathless. He could not run as fast as he used to. Many of his teammates were vaping, too. They had similar problems. Their coach was upset. He thought the kids were not working hard enough. He had no idea that they struggled to breathe because they were vaping. The e-cigarettes were small enough that kids could sneak them around without adults noticing.

When Connor went to college, he felt pressure to do well. His professors assigned a lot of work. It was hard. Whenever he felt stressed, he turned to vaping. Connor soon realized he had a problem. He wanted the nicotine too much. He needed it.

Connor decided to keep his e-cigarette in his room to limit how often he used it. Between classes, he biked back to his dorm to take a quick puff. His social life started to suffer because he rarely wanted to leave his room. If he did not vape, he felt grouchy. He often snapped at his friends.

Connor hung a piece of Velcro next to his bed and stuck his e-cigarette to it. Now he could take a puff as soon as he woke up every morning. His craving for e-cigarettes controlled his life.

TARGETING TEENS

The legal age to buy e-cigarettes is at least 21 in the United States. Many teens break the law and find ways to get them before they reach the legal age. E-cigarette companies try hard to attract young customers. They offer flavored e-juice to make the taste of e-cigarettes more appealing. Many teens say they vape because they enjoy the flavors. The companies make false claims that some flavors are healthy. The earlier people get addicted to nicotine, the more money the companies make.

▲ **The nicotine in e-cigarettes can affect a person's memory and concentration.**

When his friends said they wanted to try vaping, Connor urged them not to start. He could not stop and did not want his friends to become addicted, too.

That summer, Connor went home to work for his father's construction company. He left his e-cigarette in his bedroom so his father would not find out he was vaping. Going without vaping all day was hard.

One day when Connor was at work, his mom found the e-cigarette in his bedroom. His parents were angry and upset. They knew nicotine was very addictive.

▲ **Many e-cigarettes are small, which makes them easy for users to hide.**

Connor's parents told him that he had to stop. Connor realized he also wanted to stop. He just did not know how.

He tried to wean himself gradually from vaping. He took fewer and shorter puffs. His body quickly felt the effects of nicotine withdrawal. Connor was anxious and jittery. His limbs shook. Sometimes he curled up in a ball on his bed.

After three weeks of not vaping, the withdrawal symptoms started to go away. Connor no longer felt like he needed e-cigarettes to get through his day. Connor's friends continued to vape. Every time he was around them, he was tempted to do it, too. But he forced himself to keep saying no. He would not let himself start vaping again.

CHAPTER TWO

FROM SMOKING TO VAPING

Mark wished he had never lit his first cigarette. He hated being a smoker. He hated the stale smell that clung to his clothes and hair. He hated the smoker's cough that rattled in his chest. But he was addicted to the nicotine in cigarettes. Whenever he tried to quit, the craving for nicotine was too strong. He wanted to stop smoking, but he did not know how.

One day, Mark saw a billboard outside his office with an advertisement for e-cigarettes. He knew they contained nicotine just as real cigarettes did. And he had heard that they contained fewer harmful chemicals. However, the chemicals in e-cigarettes were still toxic. Cigarette smoking had many known risks, including cancer and heart disease. But e-cigarettes were new enough that scientists had not studied their effects. Scientists did not know how they affected people over long periods of time.

◄ **Some vape stores sell tobacco products to appeal to both smokers and vapers.**

While the risks of vaping were unknown, some people believed it was safer than smoking.

Mark knew vaping would not be good for him, but he thought it would be better than smoking. Mark bought an e-cigarette and tried it. He liked it much better than cigarettes. The vapor tasted like vanilla. It had no odor. Smoking one cigarette took several minutes. But he could puff his e-cigarette for as long or short a time as he wanted.

Soon, Mark was an ex-smoker. Now he was a vaper. Mark would vape anywhere he wanted. He did this even if it was not allowed. He hid his e-cigarette so he would not get caught.

When Mark smoked cigarettes, he had smoked mainly in the evenings and on Saturdays. Now he would vape whenever he felt the slightest craving. He could not help it. When his boss yelled at him over a missed deadline, he vaped. When he argued with his girlfriend, he vaped. He vaped when he felt stressed, and he vaped when he felt happy. Eventually, he was doing it throughout the day, every day.

Mark noticed that he was panting whenever he walked up a flight of stairs. He felt tired and breathless most of the time. He realized vaping was to blame.

Vaping can cause fluid to build up in a user's lungs, ▶ which can make physical activity difficult.

▲ Many people who use e-cigarettes were once smokers.

CHAPTER THREE

A COSTLY HABIT

Lauren closed the door to her bedroom and locked it. She took a quick puff from her e-cigarette. Her phone kept vibrating with texts from her friends. They all wanted to know why she was not at cheerleading practice. Lauren tossed her phone aside without replying. They would find out soon enough that she had quit the team. She was sick of staying after school every day. Lauren just wanted to come straight home and chill in her room with the e-cigarette that her older friends had gotten for her.

Lauren opened her closet door and started pulling clothes off hangers. Last week, she had sold a pair of boots to pay for her vaping habit. Now she needed more money. She took out a dress that was a little too tight and stuffed it into her backpack. She added a few pairs of pants and a leather skirt her mom had bought for her birthday last year. Lauren felt a twinge of regret.

◄ **After buying an e-cigarette, people must also pay for e-juice refills.**

▲ Flavored e-juice contains chemicals that may be harmful.

She loved that skirt, but she did not wear it often. And she was desperate for cash. E-cigarette **cartridges** were now costing her $150 every week. Other people she knew only spent around $15 a week. She tried to cut back, but it was not working.

The e-juice, found in the cartridges Lauren used, had high concentrations of nicotine. Whenever Lauren tried to go too long without vaping, she felt awful. Her head hurt, and everything seemed to get on her nerves. She would often snap at her friends.

Lauren and her parents were barely talking at all. They had no idea she was vaping. They were worried about Lauren's grades, which had always been good. Now Lauren was failing math and social studies. She did not want to admit it was hard to focus in school because her body craved nicotine. She would sneak out of class every day to vape in the bathroom.

Lauren felt as though the whole world was against her. She did not realize her addiction was the cause of her problems with her friends, family, and teachers.

After vaping at her boyfriend's house one day, Lauren suddenly felt very strange. Her knees became weak. She fell to the ground. Her whole body began to shake uncontrollably.

DISCOVERING THE DANGER

Researchers are still discovering the health effects of vaping. It can cause breathing problems and may worsen asthma. It also makes users more likely to get sick with colds and other illnesses. There is some evidence that vaping can cause **seizures**. As of late 2019, more than 2,000 people reported lung injuries that were connected to e-cigarette use. More than 30 people had died.

▲ **Large doses of nicotine can cause many problems including dizziness, seizures, and nausea.**

Lauren's boyfriend watched in horror as Lauren had a seizure. He called 911. An ambulance took her to the hospital.

Lauren could no longer hide from her parents that she had been vaping. They were very worried about her health. Doctors looked for an illness that could have caused her seizure. They did not find one. Her mom searched the internet and found evidence that vaping could be connected to seizures. She was convinced it had caused Lauren's.

Lauren's parents realized that their daughter had a serious problem. They wanted to help her. They gave her a choice.

Lauren could go to an addiction **rehabilitation** (rehab) program to help her quit. If she did not, she would have to leave their home. Lauren screamed and cried when they told her. She did not want to go, but she knew it was the better option for her.

Rehab was hard. Lauren craved nicotine badly. She felt symptoms of withdrawal for the first two weeks. She had painful headaches and stomachaches. She needed medicine to help her sleep.

Lauren spent most of her days in group therapy sessions. She was told what to do and when to do it. She was angry and lonely. At first, she did not want to talk to anybody. But eventually she missed her home, her family, and her friends.

After about three weeks, Lauren started to realize she was feeling more like her old self. The worst withdrawal symptoms had passed. When her parents called, she enjoyed talking to them for the first time in a long time. She spent more time thinking about school, her friends, and her future. After 40 days in rehab, she was able to go home.

Now that she had stopped vaping, Lauren was glad she went to rehab. She started seeing her old friends again. She returned to cheerleading. She would always have to fight the temptation of e-cigarettes, but she finally had her life back.

CHAPTER FOUR

EXPLOSIVE VAPING

Kayla stood in her kitchen, making lunch. As she moved around, she felt the e-cigarette in her pocket. She decided to take a quick puff. Kayla reached for her pants pocket. Suddenly, there was a loud boom. A blast sent her stumbling backward. Sparks and flames erupted from her pocket. Kayla screamed and swatted at her leg. She dropped to the ground and rolled to put out the flames. When she looked at her pants, there was a huge hole where her pocket had been. Her leg stung with a pain she had never felt in her life.

Kayla's brother ran into the kitchen. He had heard the blast. He looked at his sister and then at the shattered e-cigarette on the floor. Its battery lay a couple feet away and was still on fire. He grabbed the fire extinguisher to put out the flames. Kayla was in a daze. She was struggling to understand what had happened.

◄ **E-cigarette batteries need to be charged. Overcharging them or using the wrong charger can cause them to explode.**

Kayla's mom rushed into the kitchen, too. She saw her daughter lying on the floor, and her son kept yelling, "It blew up!" Kayla was holding her leg. It was badly burned. She was crying so hard that she could not speak. Her mom rushed to her. She then grabbed her phone and called 911. While they waited for the ambulance to arrive, Kayla's mom wrapped the burn loosely in a bandage. The paramedics came and took Kayla to the hospital.

The doctors treated Kayla's burns. She had third- and second-degree burns. Third-degree burns are the worst kind. They mean that all layers of the skin are burned. Kayla would need surgery for these burns to heal. Second-degree burns hurt only some of the skin's layers. Part of Kayla's leg had these burns, and these stung the most. The burns had been caused by Kayla's exploding e-cigarette.

Kayla was in shock. She could not believe her e-cigarette had hurt her so badly. It would take a few weeks before her second-degree burns would heal. And it would take even longer for her to recover from her third-degree burns. She was constantly in pain, and her leg would probably scar.

When she left the hospital, Kayla wanted to learn more about what had happened to her and why. She discovered that e-cigarette explosions were rare. But they had happened before.

Injuries from an e-cigarette explosion ▶ need immediate treatment.

▲ Vaping products come with warnings that they contain nicotine, but they do not warn about potential injuries.

In one state, a girl had been injured when an e-cigarette exploded in the pocket of someone sitting nearby. In another state, a boy was blinded in one eye when an e-cigarette exploded in his face. A Texas man died when metal from his exploding e-cigarette tore an artery in his neck. Researchers thought bad batteries were probably to blame for these incidents.

Kayla realized that she had been lucky to recover with only a few scars. When her leg was healed, she was happy to wear her favorite pair of jeans. But there was one thing she never wanted to put in her pocket. She promised herself she would never vape again.

THINK ABOUT IT

▶ How can vaping affect people's relationships?
▶ Why do you think e-cigarette companies focus on getting teens to start vaping?
▶ Why do you think so many people start vaping, even though it is bad for their health?

GLOSSARY

addictive (uh-DIK-tiv): An addictive substance makes people want to keep using it after they begin taking it. Nicotine is extremely addictive.

aerosol (AIR-uh-sol): An aerosol is a cloud of tiny solid or liquid particles suspended in a gas. People who vape inhale an aerosol.

cartridges (KAR-trij-iz): Cartridges are containers that are inserted into another object. Cartridges hold the e-juice that turns into an aerosol.

cravings (KRAY-vingz): Cravings are uncontrollable desires to have something. Nicotine cravings are difficult to resist.

euphoria (yoo-FOR-ee-uh): Euphoria is an intense feeling of happiness. Many drugs cause the user to experience euphoria.

nicotine (NIK-uh-teen): Nicotine is a toxic and addictive chemical found in tobacco. Most e-cigarettes contain nicotine.

rehabilitation (ree-uh-bil-uh-TAY-shun): Drug rehabilitation is a type of treatment for drug abuse. Most rehabilitation centers have strict rules for patients.

seizures (SEE-zhurz): Seizures are the shaking of the body due to abnormal electrical activity in the brain. Drug use can cause seizures.

vapor (VAY-pur): A vapor is a gas that used to be liquid or solid. People call the aerosol in e-cigarettes a vapor.

withdrawal (with-DRAW-uhl): Withdrawal is the experience of physical and mental effects when a person stops taking an addictive drug. Nicotine withdrawal causes symptoms such as irritability.

TO LEARN MORE

BOOKS

Alexander, Richard. *What's Drug Abuse?*
New York, NY: KidHaven Publishing, 2019.

Bass, Elissa. *E-cigarettes: The Risks of Addictive Nicotine and Toxic Chemicals*. New York, NY: Cavendish Square Publishing, 2016.

Idzikowski, Lisa. *The Dangers of Vaping*.
New York, NY: PowerKids Press, 2020.

WEBSITES

Visit our website for links about addiction to e-cigarettes: **childsworld.com/links**

Note to Parents, Teachers, and Librarians: We routinely verify our Web links to make sure they are safe and active sites. So encourage your readers to check them out!

SELECTED BIBLIOGRAPHY

Belluz, Julia. "Vaping May Be More Dangerous Than We Realized." *Vox*, 10 July 2019, vox.com. Accessed 3 Oct. 2019.

Campbell, Leah. "Juuling: The Addictive New Vaping Trend Teens Are Hiding." *Healthline*, 31 May 2019, healthline.com. Accessed 3 Oct. 2019.

"Nicotine & Addiction." *Smokefree Teen*, n.d., teen.smokefree.gov. Accessed 3 Oct. 2019.

INDEX

addiction, 4–5, 9–10, 13, 17, 21, 23

batteries, 4, 25, 29
breathlessness, 8, 14, 21
burns, 26

cancer, 4, 13
cartridges, 20
chemicals, 4, 13
cost, 20
cravings, 5, 9, 13, 14, 17, 21, 23

danger, 7, 17, 21

e-juice, 4, 9, 20
euphoria, 7

headaches, 20, 23
heart disease, 4, 13

injuries, 4, 21, 26, 29

legal age, 9

nicotine, 4–5, 9–11, 13, 17, 20–21, 23

quitting, 5, 13, 17, 23

rehabilitation, 23

seizures, 21–22
stress, 9, 14

taste, 7, 9, 14, 17

weaning, 11
withdrawal, 5, 11, 23

ABOUT THE AUTHOR

Jeanne Marie Ford is an Emmy-winning TV scriptwriter who holds a master of fine arts degree in writing for children from Vermont College. She has written numerous children's books and articles. Ford also teaches college English. She lives in Maryland with her husband and two children.

ADVANCES IN THE BIOSCIENCES

Volume 35

AMINOPYRIDINES AND SIMILARLY ACTING DRUGS
Effects on Nerves, Muscles and Synapses

ADVANCES IN THE BIOSCIENCES

Latest volumes in the series:

Volume 20: PERIPHERAL DOPAMINERGIC RECEPTORS
Editors: J.-L. Imbs and I. Schwartz

Volume 21: PHARMACOLOGICAL STATES OF ALERTNESS
Editors: P. Passouant and I. Oswald

Volume 22/23: MARIHUANA: BIOLOGICAL EFFECTS
Editors: G. G. Nahas and W. D. M. Paton

Volume 24: CYCLIC NUCLEOTIDES AND THERAPEUTIC PERSPECTIVES
Editors: G. Cehovic and G. A. Robison

Volume 25: THE DEVELOPMENT OF RESPONSIVENESS TO STEROID HORMONES
Editors: A. M. Kaye and M. Kaye

Volume 26: OVARIAN CANCER
Editors: C. E. Newman, C. H. J. Ford and J. A. Jordan

Volume 27: GASTROINTESTINAL EMERGENCIES 2
Editors: F. R. Barany, R. Shields and R. Caprilli

Volume 28: RECENT ADVANCES IN THE CHRONOBIOLOGY OF ALLERGY AND IMMUNOLOGY
Editors: M. H. Smolensky, A. Reinberg and J. P. McGovern

Volume 29: MELATONIN—CURRENT STATUS AND PERSPECTIVES
Editors: N. Birau and W. Schloot

Volume 30: NIGHT AND SHIFT WORK: BIOLOGICAL AND SOCIAL ASPECTS
Editors: A. Reinberg, N. Vieux and P. Andlauer

Volume 31: RECENT ADVANCES IN NEUROPSYCHOPHARMACOLOGY
Editors: B. Angrist, G. D. Burrows, M. Lader, O. Lingjaerde, G. Sedvall and D. Wheatley

Volume 32: GASTRIC CANCER
Editors: J. W. L. Fielding, C. E. Newman, C. H. J. Ford and B. G. Jones

Volume 33: ADVANCES IN HISTAMINE RESEARCH
Editors: B. Uvnäs and K. Tasaka

Volume 34: NON-STEROIDAL REGULATORS IN REPRODUCTIVE BIOLOGY AND MEDICINE
Editors: T. Fujii and C. P. Channing

Volume 35: AMINOPYRIDINES AND SIMILARLY ACTING DRUGS: Effects on Nerves, Muscles and Synapses
Editors: P. Lechat, S. Thesleff and W. C. Bowman

AMINOPYRIDINES AND SIMILARLY ACTING DRUGS
Effects on Nerves, Muscles and Synapses

Proceedings of a IUPHAR Satellite Symposium in conjunction with the 8th International Congress of Pharmacology, Paris, France, July 27-29, 1981

Organizing Committee

LEMEIGNAN *(C.N.R.S. Paris, France)*
J. MOLGO *(C.N.R.S. Paris, France)*

Editors

P. LECHAT *(Paris, France)*
S. THESLEFF *(Lund, Sweden)*
W. C. BOWMAN *(Glasgow, U.K.)*

PERGAMON PRESS
OXFORD · NEW YORK · TORONTO · SYDNEY · PARIS · FRANKFURT

U.K.	Pergamon Press Ltd., Headington Hill Hall, Oxford OX3 0BW, England
U.S.A.	Pergamon Press Inc., Maxwell House, Fairview Park, Elmsford, New York 10523, U.S.A.
CANADA	Pergamon Press Canada Ltd., Suite 104, 150 Consumers Rd., Willowdale, Ontario M2J 1P9, Canada
AUSTRALIA	Pergamon Press (Aust.) Pty. Ltd., P.O. Box 544, Potts Point, N.S.W. 2011, Australia
FRANCE	Pergamon Press SARL, 24 rue des Ecoles, 75240 Paris, Cedex 05, France
FEDERAL REPUBLIC OF GERMANY	Pergamon Press GmbH, 6242 Kronberg-Taunus, Hammerweg 6, Federal Republic of Germany

Copyright © 1982 Pergamon Press Ltd.

All Rights Reserved. No part of this publication may be reproduced, stored in a retrieval system or transmitted in any form or by any means: electronic, electrostatic, magnetic tape, mechanical, photocopying, recording or otherwise, without permission in writing from the publishers.

First edition 1982

Library of Congress Cataloging in Publication Data

Aminopyridines & similarly acting drugs.
  (Advances in the biosciences; v. 35)
  Includes index.
  1. Aminopyridines—Physiological effect—
Congresses. 2. Neuropharmacology—Congresses.
I. Lechat, P. II. Thesleff, S. (Stephen)
III. Bowman, W. C. (William Cameron) IV. International Union of Pharmacology. V. International Congress of Pharmacology (8th: 1981: Paris, France) VI. Title: Aminopyridines and similarly acting drugs. VII. Series. [DNLM:
1. Aminopyridines—Pharmacodynamics—Congresses.
2. Nervous system—Drug effects—Congresses.
3. Muscles—Drug effects—Congresses.
4. Neural transmission—Drug effects—Congresses. W3 AD244 v. 35 1981 / QU 60 A518 1981]
RM666. A465A44 1982   615'.78   82-533
AACR2

British Library Cataloguing in Publication Data

Aminopyridines & similarly acting drugs.
1. Neuropharmacology—Congresses
2. Aminopyridines—Congresses
I. Lechat, P. II. Thesleff, S. III. Bowman, W.C.
615'.78   QP346.7
ISBN 0-08-028000-5

In order to make this volume available as economically and as rapidly as possible the authors' typescripts have been reproduced in their original forms. This method unfortunately has its typographical limitations but it is hoped that they in no way distract the reader.

Printed in Great Britain by A. Wheaton & Co. Ltd., Exeter

PREFACE

When I suggested to my colleagues William Bowman and Stephen Thesleff that we organize a Symposium dedicated to aminopyridines and related compounds, they were immediately enthusiastic in supporting my proposal. We all three agreed indeed that such derivatives have provided an ever increasing interest in neurophysiology and neuropharmacology in the last twenty five years. Fortunately our project rapidly received support from all of the colleagues we contacted in order to deliver lectures.

Many scientists all round the world have published papers using aminopyridines as tools for investigating ionic channel properties and the mechanisms involved in neurotransmission at different levels: neuromuscular junction, as well as central and autonomic synapses. Moreover was it not a wonder to have such a simple chemical with such a powerful activity, therefore so very tempting for all those engaged in structure-activity relationship studies? Some new therapeutic perspectives have also been opened by these derivatives. It seemed therefore useful to have a meeting where workers, old pioneers as well as young researchers, could present their results and discuss all together. The two-and-a-half day Symposium that took place in Paris in July 1981 seems to have achieved this aim. Like all scientific meetings of limited size, it enabled its one hundred participants to have personal contacts and lay fundations for future fruitful collaboration between laboratories. The contributions of participants from 25 countries comprised an up-to-date review of present knowledge and hopefully served to stimulate future research.

The present Proceedings have been organized in eight sections according to the original Scientific Programme. They include the full papers of invited Lectures, Abstracts of oral Communications and Posters presented. The available discussions have been added after the respective scientific sessions. In order to achieve a rapid publication of these Proceedings, the texts have been prepared directly by the authors which are fully responsible for their camera-ready typescripts.

Finally, it is a pleasure to acknowledge my indebtedness to my collaborators Drs. Madeleine Lemeignan and Jordi Molgo for their untiring efforts in preparing the meeting as well as these Proceedings. I wish also to thank the technicians and secretary of my laboratory Mrs. Chantal Angeli, Mrs. Jeanine Josso, Mrs. Nicole Lettéron and Miss Annic Rodallec for their valuable assistance in preparing the meeting and during the scientific sessions.

Let me hope that the reading of these Proceedings will provide the best justification for this Symposium, opening the way to another one in a few years...

PAUL LECHAT

ACKNOWLEDGEMENTS

The Organizers wish to express their gratitude for donations received from the pharmaceutical firms listed below:

Allard, Boots-Dacour, Bristol-Meyers, Pharmuka, Merck-Sharp & Dohme-Chibret, Rhône Poulenc Santé.

Anphar-Rolland, Ciba-Geigy, Delagrange, Pierre Fabre S.A., Fournier S.A., Ipsen-Beaufour, "Produits Roche S.A., Riker, Sandoz, Sanofi, Searle, Servier, Unicet, Winthrop.

Bayer-Pharma, Beecham-Sévigné, Clin-Midi, Janssen-Le Brun, Manceau S.A., Synthélabo S.A., Innothéra, Théramex.

CONTENTS

LIST OF PARTICIPANTS   xiii

SCIENTIFIC SESSIONS*

Historical review   3
  P. Lechat

AMINOPYRIDINES AND IONIC CURRENTS IN EXCITABLE MEMBRANES

General review on potassium currents in exitable membranes of nerve and muscle   11
  H. Meves

Effects of aminopyridines on potassium currents of the nodal membrane   29
  W. ULBRICHT, H.-H. WAGNER and *J. SCHMIDTMAYER*

Properties and physiological roles of K^+ currents in frog myelinated nerve fibres as revealed by 4-aminopyridine   43
  J.M. DUBOIS

Effects of aminopyridines on ionic currents and ionic channel noise in unmyelinated axons   53
  Y. PICHON, H. MEVES and *M. PELHATE*

3- and 4-aminopyridine in synaptic transmission at the squid giant synapse   69
  R. LLINÁS, K. WALTON, M. SUGIMORI and *S. SIMON*

Discussion   81

---

*Names of presenters are underlined.

AMINOPYRIDINES AND SYNAPTIC TRANSMISSION

Lectures

General principles of synaptic transmission   87
S. THESLEFF

Effects of aminopyridines on neuromuscular transmission   95
J. MOLGO

Effects of 4-aminopyridine on transmission in excitatory and inhibitory synapses in the spinal cord   117
E. JANKOWSKA

The influence of 4-aminopyridine on parasympathetic transmission   127
F.F. FOLDES, Y. OHTA, Y. SHIWAKU, E.S. VIZI, J.J. Van DIJK and K. MORITA

Discussion   141

AMINOPYRIDINES AND THE RELEASE OF CHEMICAL TRANSMITTERS: CONTRAST WITH APAMIN

Lectures

Structure-activity relationships amongst aminopyridines   145
I.G. MARSHALL

Aminopyridine as a tool to investigate the mechanism of acetylcholine release at the nerve electroplaque junction   163
Y. DUNANT, F. CLOSTRE, G.J. JONES, F. LOCTIN and D. MULLER

Intramembrane particles changes: a constant feature of the release mechanism   173
M. ISRAEL, R. MANARANCHE, B. LESBATS and T. GULIK-KRZYWICKI

Effect of aminopyridine and related drugs on catecholamine release   183
S.M. KIRPEKAR, M.T. SCHIAVONE and J.C. PRAT

Some differences in the blockade of potassium permeabilities by apamin and the aminopyridines   199
D.H. JENKINSON

Discussion   207

MISCELLANEOUS ACTIONS OF AMINOPYRIDINES AND RELATED COMPOUNDS: POSTER COMMUNICATIONS

The action of morphine dependence on the convulsive effect of 4-aminopyridine and other drugs   211
V. ALEMAN ALEMAN and D. MARTINEZ DE MUNOZ

Antagonism to dopaminergic stereotypy, and convulsant and hypertensive effects by 2-amino-4-methylpyridine   212
F. BERGMANN

Contents

4-aminopyridine (4AP) enhances acetylcholine output from the rat cerebral cortex *in vivo* — 213
  R. CORRADETTI, P. MANTOVANI, K. LÖFFELHOLZ and G. PEPEU

4-aminopyridine as a tool to elucidate different actions of botulinum A and tetanus toxin at the mouse neuromuscular junction — 214
  F. DREYER and A. SCHMITT

Antagonism of the myoneural activity of antibiotics, local anesthetics and general anesthetics by 4-APYR — 215
  F.F. FOLDES, D.B.S. RAO, K. THOMAS, I. LEUNG, G. BIKHAZI and H. NAGASHIMA

Increased tetanic fade produced by 3,4-diaminopyridine in the presence of neuromuscular blocking agents — 216
  A.J. GIBB, I.G. MARSHALL and W.C. BOWMAN

Effect of 4-aminopyridine on the electrical activity of the hippocampus and the cerebellum — 217
  G. GOGOLÁK, K. CZECH and Ch. STUMPF

Cardiac effects of 4-aminoquinoline on mammalian and amphibian isolated preparations. An electrophysiological study — 218
  S. GUERRERO, L. NOVAKOVIC, J. CAMPOS and M. PENNA

Facilitatory effects of aminopyridines on synaptic transmission in the sixth abdominal ganglion of the cockroach — 219
  B. HUE, M. PELHATE, J.J. CALLEC and J. CHANELET

The effect of 3-, 4-AP and 3,4-DAP on the evoked activity of the pyramidal cell layer (CA 1,2) of the hippocampus. An *in vitro* study — 220
  U. KUHNT and Magdolna SZENTE

Fast and slow automatic activity of squid giant axons induced by 4-aminopyridine — 221
  E. LAMMEL and K. MANDREK

The ability of 4-AP and 3,4-DAP to cross the blood-brain barrier can account for their difference in toxicity — 222
  M. LEMEIGNAN, H. MILLART, N. LETTERON, D. LAMIABLE, J. JOSSO, H. CHOISY and P. LECHAT

Action of 4AP and TEA on presynaptic currents in mammalian motor endings — 223
  A. MALLART and J.L. BRIGANT

Protein synthesis in brain subcellular fractions. Effect of 4-aminopyridine — 224
  D. MARTINEZ DE MUNOZ

Effects of 4-hydroxypyridine on transmitter release at the neuromuscular junction — 225
  G. MONTOYA, J. MOLGO, M. LEMEIGNAN and P. LECHAT

4-aminopyridine analogs of novel chemical structure — 226
  Y. OHTA, I. CHAUDHRY, I. LALEZARI and F.F. FOLDES

Excitatory action of imidazole on evoked transmitter release from the phrenic nerve and on potassium-stimulated ^{45}Ca uptake by synaptosomes in the rat — 227
J.A. RIBEIRO, M.L. DOMINGUEZ and A.M. SÁ-ALMEIDA

Aminopyridine effects on molecular models in myopathic states — 228
G.K. ROUSSEV, D. PASKOV and T. JIRKOLOVA

Effects of pyridine on the frog rectus abdominis muscle — 229
M.J. ROWAN and P.L. CHAMBERS

4-aminopyridine and presynaptic modulation of transmitter release in *Aplysia* — 230
T. SHIMAHARA

Naloxone, 4-aminopyridine and physostigmine as antagonists of morphine in rabbits — 231
R.L. SIA, P. WESTRA and H. WESSELING

Anti-curare action of 4-aminopyridine and 4-aminopyridine-like substances — 232
V. SOBEK

4-aminopyridine reversal of morphine analgesia — 233
A.S. TUNG and B.W. BRANDOM

4-aminopyridine as antagonist of the cardiovascular and neuromuscular depressant effects of kanamycin in rats — 234
T. UCHIYAMA, M. LEMEIGNAN and P. LECHAT

FURTHER ACTIONS OF AMINOPYRIDINES ON MUSCLE AND NERVE: SHORT COMMUNICATIONS

Effects of 4-aminopyridine on mammalian peripheral and central neurones — 237
M. GALVAN, P. GRAFE and G. ten BRUGGENCATE

Interactions of aminopyridines and related compounds with ionic channels in the isolated cockroach axon — 238
M. PELHATE, B. HUE, Y. PICHON and J. CHANELET

4-aminopyridine-induced alteration in the receptive field of cuneate and gracile neurones — 239
N.E. SAADE, N.R. BANNA, A.J. KHOURY, S.J. JABBUR and P.D. WALL

Effect of 4-aminopyridine on the desensitisation of the rat diaphragm caused by carbachol — 240
O. VITAL BRAZIL and M.D. FONTANA

The effects of 4-aminopyridine on neuromuscular block produced by succinyldicholine — 241
N.N. DURANT, C. LEE and R.L. KATZ

Chemical modulators: their molecular characteristics and kinetics of actions — 242
T. MAENO

Discussion — 243

AMINOPYRIDINES AND SKELETAL, SMOOTH AND CARDIAC MUSCLE

Lectures

Effects of 4-aminopyridine on contractile properties of skeletal muscle — 249
  K.A.P. EDMAN and *A.R. KHAN*

Effects of 4-aminopyridine on cardiac muscle — 261
  T. YANAGISAWA and *N. TAIRA*

Oral communications

Effects of 4-aminopyridine on isometric force - [Ca^{++}] - relations in mammalian slow and fast twitch skinned muscle fibres — 275
  R. FINK and *D.G. STEPHENSON*

4-aminopyridine and outward membrane currents in rat uterine smooth muscle at various stages of pregnancy — 276
  J.P. SAVINEAU, J. MIRONNEAU and *Ch. MIRONNEAU*

Effects of 4-aminopyridine on membrane currents in the pace-maker voltage range of sheep cardiac Purkinje fibres — 277
  P.P. Van BOGAERT

Is the cardiotonic effect of aminopyridines and aminopyrimidines *in vitro* a consequence of increased extracellular pH? — 278
  M. SHAHID and *I.W. RODGER*

Discussion — 279

CLINICAL APPLICATIONS OF AMINOPYRIDINES

Lectures

Therapeutic applications of aminopyridines in diseases of neuromuscular transmission — 287
  H. LUNDH

Use of 4-aminopyridine in human botulism — 297
  A.P. BALL, M. SNOW and *R. PAUL*

Therapeutic applications of 4-aminopyridine in anaesthesia — 303
  S. AGOSTON, D.R.A. UGES and *R.L. SIA*

Oral communications

Effects of 3,4-diaminopyridine in Cynomolgus monkeys poisoned with type A botulinum toxin — 313
  G.E. LEWIS and *R.M. WOOD*

Discussion — 315

FURTHER MISCELLANEOUS ACTIONS OF AMINOPYRIDINES AND RELATED COMPOUNDS: SHORT COMMUNICATIONS

Oral communications

Potassium channel block by S-methylthiouronium, a pharmacological analogue of 4-aminopyridine ... 321
F.N. FASTIER, M. PELHATE and *B. HUE*

Differences in actions of 4-aminopyridine and 4-methyl-2-aminopyridine ... 322
W.E. GLOVER

Effects of aminopyridines in avian muscular dystrophy ... 323
P.J. BARNARD, E.A. BARNARD and *E.S. ALLAN*

Comparison of the actions of dendrotoxin, a facilitatory neurotoxin, and 3,4-diaminopyridine on neuromuscular transmission ... 324
A.L. HARVEY

Effects of aminopyridines on parasympathetic neuroeffector transmission in the heart ... 325
W. WEIDE, R. LINDMAR and *K. LÖFFELHOLZ*

Effects of 4-aminopyridine on endocrine cells ... 326
O. SAND, K. HOVE, S. OZAWA, K. GAUTVIK and *E. HAUG*

An electroencephalographic study of 4-aminopyridine in conscious volunteers ... 327
R.L. SIA, S. BOONSTRA, P. WESTRA, H.T.M. HAENEN and *H. WESSELING*

Discussion ... 329

Conclusions ... 335
W.C. BOWMAN

INDEX ... 343

LIST OF PARTICIPANTS

AGOSTON Sandor, Department of Anaesthesiology, University Hospital, Oostersingel 59, 9700 RB Groningen, The Netherlands.
BALL A. Peter, Infectious Diseases Unit, Cameron Hospital, Windygates, Fife, KY 8 5RR, United Kingdom.
BARNARD Eric A., Department of Biochemistry, Imperial College of Sciences and Technology, London SW 7, United Kingdom.
BARNARD Penelope J., Department of Biochemistry, Imperial College of Sciences and Technology, London SW 7, U.K.
BERGMAN Claude, Laboratoire de Neurobiologie, Ecole Normale Supérieure, 46, rue d'Ulm, 75230 Paris Cedex 05, France.
BERGMANN Félix, Department of Pharmacology, The Hebrew University, Hadassah Medical School, Jerusalem 91000, Israël.
van BOGAERT Pierre-Paul, Laboratorium voor Fysiologie, Universiteit Antwerpen, RUCA, Groenenborgerlaan 171, B 2020 Antwerpen, Belgium.
BOWMAN William C., Department of Physiology and Pharmacology, University of Strathclyde, George Street 204, Glasgow G1 1XW, Scotland, United Kingdom.
BRANDOM Barbara W., Department of Anesthesiology, Children's Hospital of Pittsburgh, 125 de Soto Street, Pittsburgh, PA 15213, U.S.A.
BRIGANT Jean-Louis, Laboratoire de Neurobiologie cellulaire, C.N.R.S., 91190 Gif sur Yvette, France.
CHANELET Jean, Laboratoire de Physiologie, U.E.R. de Sciences Médicales et Pharmaceutiques, 49045 Angers Cedex, France.
CORRADETTI Renato, Istituto Interfacolta di Farmacologia e Tossicologia della Universita di Firenze, Viale G.B. Morgagni 65, 50134 Firenze, Italia.
COUTEAUX René, Laboratoire de Cytologie, Université Pierre et Marie Curie, 7, Quai Saint-Bernard, 75230 Paris Cedex 05, France.
DUBOIS Jean-Marc, Laboratoire de Neurobiologie, Ecole Normale Supérieure, 46, rue d'Ulm, 75230 Paris Cedex 05, France.
DUNANT Yves, Département de Pharmacologie, Ecole de Médecine, rue de l'Ecole de Médecine 20, 1211 Genève 4, Switzerland.
DURANT Nicholas, Department of Anesthesiology, University of California, UCLA, School of Medicine, Los Angeles, CA 90024, U.S.A.
EDMAN K.A.Paul, Department of Pharmacology, University of Lund, Sölvegatan 10, S 223 62 Lund, Sweden.
FARINE Dan, Ambassade d'Israël, 3, rue Rabelais, 75008 Paris, France.
FASTIER Frederic Noël, Department of Pharmacology, Otago University, P.O. Box 913, Dunedin, New-Zealand.
FINK Rainer H.A., Department of Zoology, La Trobe University, Bundoora, Victoria 3083, Australia.
FOLDES Francis F., Department of Anesthesiology, Montefiore Hospital and Medical Center, 111 East 210th Street, Bronx, NY 10467, U.S.A.
GALVAN Martin, Physiologisches Institut der Universität München, Pettenkoferstrasse 12, 8000 München 2, Federal Republic of Germany.
GIBB Alasdair James, Department of Physiology and Pharmacology, University of Strathclyde, Royal College, 204 George Street, Glasgow G1 1XW, Scotland, United Kingdom.
GLOVER Walter E., School of Physiology and Pharmacology, University of New South Wales, P.O. Box 1, Kensington, New South Wales 2033, Australia.
GOGOLÁK Gertrude, Institut für Neuropharmakologie, Währinger Strasse 13a, 1090 Wien, Austria.
GOMEZ Stephen, Department of Neuropathology, Institute of Neurology, The National Hospital, Queen Square, London WC 1 N, 3 BG, United Kingdom.

GRAFE Peter, Physiologisches Institut der Universität München, Pettenkoferstrasse 12, 8000 München 2, Federal Republic of Germany.
GUERRERO A. Sergio, Departamento de Farmacologia, Universidad de Chile, Casilla 16387, (P.O.Box), Santiago 9, Chile.
HARVEY Alan L., Department of Physiology and Pharmacology, University of Strathclyde, Glasgow G1 1XW, Scotland, United Kingdom.
HUE Bernard, U.E.R. de Médecine, Département de Physiologie, rue Haute de Reculée, 49045 Angers Cedex, France.
ISRAËL Maurice, Département de Biophysique et de Neurochimie, Laboratoire de Neurobiologie Cellulaire, C.N.R.S., 91190 Gif sur Yvette, France.
JANKOWSKA Elzbieta, Göteborg Universitet, Fysiologiska Institutionen, Box 33031, S 400 33 Göteborg, Sweden.
JENKINSON Donald H., Department of Pharmacology, University College London, Gower Street, London WC1E 6BT, United Kingdom.
JOURDON Philippe, Institut de Pharmacologie, 15, rue de l'Ecole de Médecine, 75006 Paris, France.
KHAN Abdur Rauf, Department of Pharmacology, University of Lund, Sölvegatan 10, S 223 62 Lund, Sweden.
KIRPEKAR Sadashiv M., State University of New York, Department of Pharmacology, Downstate Medical Center (Box 29), 450 Clarkson Avenue, Brooklyn, NY 11203, U.S.A.
KHODOROV Boris Israelovitch, A.V. Vishnevsky Surgery Institute of the Academy of Medical Sciences of the U.S.S.R., Moscow 113093, U.S.S.R.
KUHNT Ulrich, Max-Planck-Institut für Biophysikalische Chemie, D-3400 Göttingen-Nikolausberg, Postfach 968, Federal Republic of Germany.
LAMMEL Ernst, Physiologisches Institut der Philipps-Universität, Deutschhausstrasse 2, D 3550 Marburg/Lahn, Federal Republic of Germany.
LECHAT Paul, Institut de Pharmacologie, 15, rue de l'Ecole de Médecine, 75006 Paris, France.
Le FUR Gérard, Pharmindustrie, B.P. 158, 92231 Gennevilliers, France.
LEMEIGNAN Madeleine, Institut de Pharmacologie, 15, rue de l'Ecole de Médecine, 75006 Paris, France.
LEWIS George E., Pathology Division, U.S. Army Medical Research, Institute of Infectious Diseases, Fort Detrick, Frederick, MD 21701, U.S.A.
LLINAS Rodolfo, Department of Physiology and Biophysics, New York University Medical Center, 550 First Avenue, New York, NY 10016, U.S.A.
LÖFFELHOLZ Konrad, Pharmakologisches Institut der Universität Mainz, Obere Zahlbacher Strasse 67, 6500 Mainz 1, Federal Republic of Germany.
LOWY Robert, Groupe de Recherches sur la Physiopathologie de la Nutrition (U.177 INSERM), 15, rue de l'Ecole de Médecine, 75006 Paris, France.
LUNDH Hakan, Department of Neurology, University Hospital, S 221 85 Lund, Sweden.
McARDLE Joseph J., Department of Pharmacology, New Jersey Medical School, Newark, New Jersey 07103, U.S.A.
MAENO Takashi, Department of Physiology, Shimane Medical University 89-1 Enyacho, Izumo 693, Japan.
MALLART Alberto, Laboratoire de Neurobiologie Cellulaire du C.N.R.S., 91190 Gif sur Yvette, France.
MANDREK Kurt, Institut für Physiologie der Universität Marburg/Lahn, Deutschhausstrasse 2, 3550 Marburg/Lahn, Federal Republic of Germany.
MARSHALL Ian G., The University of Strathclyde, Department of Physiology and Pharmacology, Royal College, 204 George Street, Glasgow G1 1XW, Scotland, United Kingdom.
MARTINEZ de MUÑOS Dalila, Instituto Nacional Politecnico, Centro de Investigacion y de estudiantos avanzados, Departamento de Neurociencias, Appartado Postal 14-740, Mexico City 14, D.F., 5 Mexico.
MEVES Hans, I.Physiologisches Institut der Universität des Saarlandes, D 6650 Homburg/Saar, Federal Republic of Germany.

List of Participants

MILLART Hervé, Laboratoire de Pharmacologie, C.H.R., 45, rue Cognacq Jay, 51092 Reims Cedex, France.
MOLGÓ Jordi, Institut de Pharmacologie, 15, rue de l'Ecole de Médecine, 75006 Paris, France.
MONTOYA Gonzalo, Departamento de Ciencias Fisiologicas, Facultad de Ciencias Biologicas y de Recursos Naturales, Universidad de Concepcion, Concepcion, Chile.
OHTA Yoshio, Montefiore Hospital and Medical Center, Anesthesiology Research Laboratory, 111 East 120th Street, Bronx, NY 10467, U.S.A.
PASKOV Dimitri, 5, rue Razlatitza, 1463 Sofia, Bulgaria.
PECOT-DECHAVASSINE Monique, Laboratoire de Cytologie, Université Pierre et Marie Curie, 4, place Jussieu, 75230 Paris cedex 05, France.
PELHATE Marcel, U.E.R. de Médecine, Laboratoire de Physiologie, rue Haute de Reculée, 49045 Angers Cedex, France.
PERADEJORDI Federico, Centre de Mécanique Ondulatoire du C.N.R.S., 23, rue du Maroc, 75019 Paris, France.
PICHON Yves, Département de Biophysique, Laboratoire de Neurobiologie Cellulaire du C.N.R.S., 91190 Gif sur Yvette.
POLAK Robert, Medical Biological Laboratory, T.N.O., Postbox 45, 2280 AA Rijswijk, The Netherlands.
RIBEIRO Joaquim, Centro de Biologia, Instituto Gulbenkian de Ciencia, Oeiras, Portugal.
ROWAN Michael J., Department of Pharmacology, University of Dublin, Trinity College, Dublin 2, Eire.
SAADE Nayef Emile, Departement de Sciences Naturelles, Faculté des Sciences, Université Libanaise, Hadeth-Beyrouth, Liban.
SAND Olav, Department of Physiology, Veterinary College of Norway, P.O. Box 8146, Oslo 1, Norway.
SAVINEAU Jean-Pierre, Université de Bordeaux II, Institut de Biochimie Cellulaire et de Neurochimie du C.N.R.S., 1, rue Camille Saint-Saens, 33000 Bordeaux, France.
SCHIAVONE Marc, State University of New-York, Downstate Medical Center, Department of Pharmacology, Box 29, 450 Clarkson Avenue, Brooklyn, NY 11203, U.S.A.
SCHMITT Andreas, Rudolf-Buchheim Institut fuer Pharmakologie der Justus-Liebig Universitaet, Frankfurter Str. 107, D 6300 Giessen, Federal Republic of Germany.
SEBALD Madeleine, Département des Anaérobies, Institut Pasteur, 25, rue du Docteur Roux, 75015 Paris, France.
SELLIN Lawrence C., Pathology Division, Department of the Army, U.S. Army Medical Research Institute of Infectious Diseases, Fort Detrick, Frederick, MD 21701, U.S.A.
SHAHID M., Department of Physiology and Pharmacology, University of Strathclyde, George Street 204, Glasgow G1 1XW, Scotland, United Kingdom.
SHARE Norman Nathan, Laboratoire Merck, Sharp & Dohme-Chibret, Route de Marsat, B.P. 127, 63203 Riom Cedex, France.
SHIMAHARA Takeshi, Département de Biophysique, Laboratoire de Neurobiologie Cellulaire du C.N.R.S., 91190 Gif sur Yvette, France.
SOBEK Vojtech, Laboratory for the Research of Infectious Diseases, Faculty of Pediatrics, Charles University, 180 81 Prague 8, Bulovka, Czechoslovakia.
STOYANOV Emil, Department of Anaesthesiology and Resuscitation, Medical Academy, Bul. Patriarch Evitmi 59, 1463 Sofia, Bulgaria.
SZENTE Magdolna, Alsókikötö sor 5.VIII. 48, 6726 Szeged, Hungaria.
TAZIEFF-DEPIERRE France, Institut de Pharmacologie, 15, rue de l'Ecole de Médecine, 75006 Paris, France.
THESLEFF Stephen, Department of Pharmacology, University of Lund, Sölvegatan 10, S 223 62 Lund, Sweden.
UCHIYAMA Toshimitsu, Department of Pharmacology, Toho University School of Medicine, 21-16 Omori-Nishi 5 chome, Ota-Ku, Tokyo 143, Japan.
ULBRICHT Werner, Christian-Albrechts Universität zu Kiel, Physiologisches Institut, Olshausenstrasse 40/60, 2300 Kiel 1, Federal Republic of Germany.
VITAL-BRAZIL Oswaldo, Department of Pharmacology, Faculty of Medical Sciences, State University of Campinas, C.P. 1170, Campinas, Sao Paulo, Brazil.

WEIDE Wolfgang, Pharmakologisches Institut der Universität Mainz, Obere Zahlbacher Strasse 67, 6500 Mainz 1, Federal Republic of Germany.
WESTRA Pieter, Institute of Anaesthesiology, Oostersingel 59, 9713 EZ Groningen, The Netherlands.

YANAGISAWA Teruyuki, Department of Pharmacology, Tohoku University, School of Medicine, Seiryo-machi 2-1, Sendai 980, Japan.

Historical Review

1867. (June 21.) Mexico surrenders to Diaz.
1868. Diaz in retirement.
,, Overthrow of monarchy in Spain. Suez Canal completed.
1869. General Grant President of U.S.A.
1870. Franco-Prussian War and fall of the Empire.
1871. Diaz becomes leader of party which opposes re-election of Juarez.
,, Renewed civil war in Mexico.
,, (Jan. 18.) King of Prussia proclaimed German Emperor in Versailles.
,, (March 18—May 21.) Revolt of the Commune in Paris.
,, (May 10.) Treaty of Frankfort signed.
1872. (July 18.) Death of Juarez.
,, Sebastian Lerdo de Tejada interim President of Mexico.
,, Diaz submits and retires to Oaxaca.
1873. Opening of Veracruz to Mexico Railway.
,, Frontier troubles with U.S.A.
,, Unsuccessful attempts to arrange Mexican debt. Mexico resumes diplomatic relations with all Powers except Great Britain.
1874. Restoration of monarchy in Spain.
1876. Diaz heads a revolt to oppose re-election of Lerdo de Tejada.
,, (Nov. 13.) Wins decisive battle at Tecoac and is proclaimed interim President.
,, Formation of La Société Civile Internationale du Canal Interocéanique to promote construction of Panama Canal.
1877. Diaz expels J. M. Iglesias.
,, Pacifies Mexico and begins to pay indemnity to U.S.A.
,, Hayes President of U.S.A.
1878. Diaz recognised as President of Mexico by U.S.A.
,, (May 28.) The Bonaparte-Wyse concession for the construction of Panama Canal granted by Colombia.
,, (Dec.) The Veracruz massacre.